HOUNDS OF HORROR

Written and Illustrated
by Shoo Rayner

Dug's Bronze Age Family

Dug

Woof

Over 3,000 years ago, Dug's family lived in the southwest of Britain. In those days, wolves, bears and other dangerous animals roamed free. Join Dug as he learns to hunt with his new hunting partner.

Mini

Dad

Chapter One

"Throw!" yelled Dad. Three spears flew
through the air towards a herd of deer. The
creatures stood alert, ears pricked, noses
twitching, ready to run from danger.

Thud! Thud! Thud! The spears jabbed into the soft earth, falling short of their targets. The deer bent their heads and went back to eating the lush, green grass.

"It's no good," Dad whispered. "We need to get closer or we'll never eat meat again."

"But the deer keep moving," Dug sighed.

"It's so unfair!" Mini complained. "I'm only little. I can't throw my spear far enough."

"Look!" Dug warned. "There's a wolf! It's driving the deer towards us." The wolf barked. The deer panicked and ran.

Dad stood up and hurled a spear at the giant stag as it thundered towards them.

"You got him!" Mini danced around the stag that lay on the grass. It's wide eyes stared blankly at the sky.

"You did it, Dad!" Dug cheered. "That will feed us for weeks!"

Chapter Two

"Mmmm, that smells so good!" said Mini, as Dad stirred the cooking pot.

"Someone else thinks so too," Dug said, peering through a crack in the door. "That wolf is out there. Should we feed her? She looks hungry. After all, she did help us."

"NEVER trust a wolf!" said Dad. "Anyway, how do you know it was that wolf? They all look the same."

"This one is different. She doesn't howl like the other wolves," Dug added.

Outside, in the dim evening light, the wolf barked, "Ruff!"

Soon she was drowned out by the howls of
the rest of the pack.

"There you are," said Dad. "She's brought
all her friends with her. NEVER trust a wolf!"

Dug watched the lone wolf quietly slip away
into the night, while the rest of the pack
sang their mournful songs to the moon.

Chapter Three

"There's so much meat!" said Dad. "You two can take some to Granny."

"Yay!" Dug and Mini cheered. Granny always had something nice for them to eat.

"I hope she's got some honey cakes!" Dug said, licking his lips.

"Stick to the path!" Dad said. "And don't go too near the barrow. That's where the wolves meet up." Dug and Mini set off.

"The barrow looks creepy. I'm scared," said
Mini. She shivered at the grassy mound.
"Me too!" said Dug. "Just think of all the
dead people in there." Then, a sudden
movement caught Dug's eye.

"We're being followed!" Dug yelled.

"It's that wolf!" Mini whimpered. "What are
we going to do?" The wolf licked its lips and
watched them. It was no more than ten
paces away.

"I'm going to give her some meat," said Dug, throwing a piece of steak towards the animal. "She deserves it."

The wolf ripped the meat to shreds and swallowed it in three big gulps. Then she stood up, alert, ears twitching, growling deep and low. She crept towards them.

"Hold my hand and don't run," Dug whispered to Mini. The wolf was herding them, just like it herded the deer.

"More wolves!" Mini squeaked. The rest of the wolf pack appeared like ghosts, padding towards them, driving them towards the barrow!

Chapter Four

"Get inside!" Dug pushed Mini through the narrow stone entrance. The lone wolf stood her ground, protecting the children inside.

"What are we going to do?" cried Mini.

"We wait." Dug spoke in a gentle, calming

voice. "The wolf will look after us."

Mini was crying. "But Dad says we should

NEVER trust a wolf!"

"We have to," said Dug.

The wolf pack circled the barrow, howling long, hungry wails. Deep inside the barrow, the skulls of ancestors lined the walls. The lone wolf watched and waited. Mini and Dug watched and waited too.

"We're going to die!" Mini cried.

"No one will ever know we were here!"

The pack of wolves paced around the

entrance and growled.

The lone wolf stood her ground, bared her long, yellow teeth and barked a loud "Woof!" The pack stopped dead in their tracks. None of them dared attack. This wolf was brave. This wolf was fierce. This wolf was different!

Day grew into night. Dug and Mini heard the wolves above them scratching, trying to dig their way into the dark, damp chamber. Bats flew in and out, flapping and twittering around their heads.

Chapter Five

"Listen, voices! And look, torches!" said Dug.

"It's Dad!" sobbed Mini. "He's come to
save us!"

A search party had come looking for them. In the flickering torchlight, Dug saw Dad raise his arm and aim his shining bronze tipped spear at the brave, lone wolf by the doorway.

"Dad, no!" Dug stood in front of the wolf.

"You can't, Dad. She's different."

"NEVER trust a wolf!" Dad snarled. The torchlight glinted in his eyes.

"But she saved us, Dad," Dug pleaded. "We owe her our lives!"

Dad stared at the wolf, making up his mind.

"Okay," he said, lowering the spear.

"She can sleep by the door and keep watch. If she helps us, we'll feed her."

"Hooray! You can stay!" said Dug. "I will call you Woof, the loudest, bravest noise a wolf can make."

"Welcome to the family, Woof," said Dad.

"Ruff!" said Woof.

Bronze Age Facts

Bronze Age hunters used bronze spearheads and sharp bronze knives to hunt for food and protect themselves from dangerous wolves, lynxes and wild boar. Barrows were places to bury the dead. You can still see barrows in the British Isles, like West Kennet Long Barrow near Stonehenge. All pet dogs are descended from wolves. Maybe Woof is the great, great grandmother of them all!

Franklin Watts
First published in Great Britain in 2016
by The Watts Publishing Group

Text and Illustrations © Shoo Rayner 2016

Series Editor: Melanie Palmer
Series Advisor: Catherine Glavina
Series Designers: Peter Scoulding
and Cathryn Gilbert

ISBN 978 1 4451 4803 8 (hbk)
ISBN 978 1 4451 4805 2 (pbk)
ISBN 978 1 4451 4804 5 (library ebook)

Printed in China

MIX
Paper from
responsible sources

FSC
www.fsc.org
FSC® C104740

Franklin Watts
An imprint of
Hachette Children's Group
Part of The Watts Publishing Group
Carmelite House
50 Victoria Embankment
London EC4Y 0DZ

An Hachette UK Company
www.hachette.co.uk

www.franklinwatts.co.uk